MARC BROWN
ARTHUR
Turns Green

LITTLE, BROWN AND COMPANY
New York   Boston

Little, Brown and Company

Hachette Book Group
237 Park Avenue, New York, NY 10017
Visit our website at www.lb-kids.com

Little, Brown and Company is a division of
Hachette Book Group, Inc.
The Little, Brown name and logo are trademarks of Hachette Book Group, Inc.

First Edition: April 2011
Arthur ® is a registered trademark of Marc Brown

Brown, Marc Tolon.
Arthur turns green / by Marc Brown. — 1st ed.
p. cm.
Summary: When Arthur starts talking about his school project involving a Big Green Machine, D.W. imagines a scary contraption that will turn everyone green.
ISBN 978-0-316-12924-4
[1. Environmental protection—Fiction. 2. Schools—Fiction. 3. Brothers and sisters—Fiction. 4. Aardvark—Fiction.] I. Title.
PZ7.B81618Alu 2011
[E]—dc22   2010034257

10 9 8 7 6 5 4 3 2 1

QUAL

Printed in China

This book was printed in soy ink on recycled paper created from 50 percent postconsumer waste.

Arthur's class was working in the school garden when Mr. Ratburn began to explain their next class project. "Let's call it the Big Green Machine," he said. "Your job is to find ways to make our planet a better place to live. We'll present all of your ideas at a school family night."

On the way home from school, Arthur and his friends talked about their projects.

"I'm thinking garbage," said Buster, "because I love food, and when you don't eat food, it turns into garbage. So maybe I need to eat more?"

"I'm going to sell all my old clothes so other people can use them," said Muffy. "Then I can buy new clothes!"

"I'm going to collect soda cans and return them for the deposits," said Binky. "I can use the money to save polar bears."

"What's your project, Arthur?" his friends asked.

Arthur just smiled. "You'll see," he said.

At home, Arthur walked around the house making notes and talking to himself.

"Why are you acting weirder than usual?" asked D.W.

"The Big Green Machine" was all Arthur said as he unplugged his mom's cell phone charger.

After dinner, Arthur changed the lightbulbs in three lamps to bulbs that save energy. At bedtime, he took the shortest shower ever and shut the water off while he brushed his teeth.

Then Arthur came in to say good night to D.W. and turned off the lights while she was still reading *Fluffy, the Very Special Unicorn.*

The next day, Arthur and his friends stayed
after school to work on their projects.
"Is that a picture of your house?" asked Buster.
"Yes," said Arthur. "I found things I can do to
save energy in almost every room."

Arthur was late for dinner.

"You owe me big-time," said D.W. "I had to set the table, and that's *your* job."

"Sorry," said Arthur. "I had to deal with the Big Green Machine at school."

Then D.W. noticed Arthur's green hands. *That machine is turning Arthur green!* she thought.

At bedtime, D.W. found lots of new plants in her room. She heard odd noises coming from the garage. A shadowy figure was sneaking through the yard!

Things are getting really creepy around here, she thought.

The next morning at preschool, D.W. worried about Arthur.
"There's a big machine that's turning my brother green," D.W. told her friends.

"You're making that up," said Tommy and Timmy.
"Am not," said D.W. "Come over to my house after
school and see for yourselves."

Later that afternoon, Buster helped Arthur and
his dad work in the garden.
"You have a real green thumb, Arthur!" said Dad.
"Me too," joked Buster. "I'm still green from
working on our projects."

"Wow!" said Tommy. "Arthur really *is* turning green!"

"Look!" said Timmy. "So is Buster!"

"Somehow this big green machine turns everyone green," said D.W.

At dinner, Arthur set the table with cloth napkins instead of paper ones.

When his family was finished eating, he checked his watch.

"Time to go," he said.

"Go where?" asked D.W.

"Dad's helping us with the Big Green Machine at school," Arthur explained.

"See you later, alligator," said Dad.
Oh no! thought D.W. *Not Dad, too!*

That night, D.W. dreamed about a big green machine that ran around turning everyone green. Then it started chasing her. She woke up just in time!

When she went down for breakfast, D.W. gasped.
Dad's hands were green, too!
"Tonight is family night at school," said Arthur.
"I'll show you how we can have the Big Green
Machine right here at home!"
"I can't go," declared D.W. "I feel sick. Real sick."

But D.W. didn't have a temperature, so that
night the whole family went to Arthur's school.
Just before they went in, D.W. suddenly grabbed
Arthur's arm.

"Help me!" cried D.W. "I don't want the big
green machine to turn me green, too!"

"It's not what you think," said Arthur.

"Follow me."

"The Big Green Machine is just the name of our class project. It's about all the things we can do to save the planet," said Arthur.
"Oh. Well, why didn't you say so?" said D.W.
Mom smiled and gave Arthur a hug.
Then D.W. read Arthur's poster out loud.

Back at home, Dad made ice cream sundaes.
Then it was time for bed.
Arthur and D.W. turned off the water while
they brushed their teeth.
"It's so funny that you thought the Big
Green Machine was turning everyone
green." Arthur laughed.
"Yeah, that was pretty funny," agreed D.W.

Suddenly, everything went dark.
"Hey!" said Arthur. "Who turned off
the lights?"
"I did," said D.W. with a giggle.
"Looks like I'm turning green, too!"

3 1901 05000 6685